A NOTE ABOUT THE STORY

Who can resist the wonderful taste of the Italian bread *panettone*? Made with eggs, raisins and candied fruit, this cakelike bread has a strong association with the northern Italian city of Milan. And especially with the *Café Motta* situated across from the cathedral—the *Duomo*—in the world-famous *Galleria*, the elegant glass-enclosed shopping arcade where the Milanese promenade on Sunday afternoons.

Every Christmas, *Motta* sends boatloads of *panettone* to the United States so Americans can enjoy it along with their Milanese counterparts.

Like any good and unique food, *panettone* has several stories explaining its creation. The one that captured my imagination concerns a baker, his daughter and a rich young man. I have taken great liberties in this tale, except for the three wise *zie*—aunties. Everyone who knows anything about the Italians will recognize the three ladies in black who are so inseparable that they form a single silhouette.

Buona Lettura! (Good Reading!)

—*Tomie dePaola, Creative Director*
WHITEBIRD BOOKS

Tony's Bread

An Italian Folktale by

Tomie dePaola

A WHITEBIRD BOOK
G.P. Putnam's Sons
New York

For *Lon Driggers* and *Bob Sass,*
who sat there and listened
while I told them this story

Text and illustrations copyright © 1989 by Tomie dePaola
All rights reserved. Published simultaneously in Canada.
Printed in Hong Kong by South China Printing Co. (1988) Limited.
Library of Congress Cataloging-in-Publication Data
dePaola, Tomie. Tony's bread /
written & illustrated by Tomie dePaola.
p. cm. — (A Whitebird book)
Summary: A baker loses his daughter but gains a bakery
in the grand city of Milano after meeting a determined
nobleman and baking a unique loaf of bread.
[1. Bread — Folklore. 2. Folklore — Italy.] I. Title.
II. Series. PZ8.1.D43Tp 1989 88-7687
398.2′1′0945-dc19 CIP AC
ISBN 0-399-21693-6
10 9 8 7 6 5 4 3 2 1
First impression

Once, a long time ago, in a small village outside the grand city of Milano, there lived a baker named Antonio. But everyone called him Tony.

Tony made bread and only bread in his bakery. It was good and simple and the villagers loved it. But Tony had a dream. One day he would have a bakery of his own in Milano and become the most famous baker in all of northern Italy.

Now, Tony lived with his only daughter, Serafina. He was a widower and he had raised Serafina from the time she was *una piccola bambina*—a little girl. And how he had spoiled her!

"Antonio treats Serafina like *una principessa*"—a princess— said Zia Clotilda.

"The finest clothes, the finest jewelry, anything her heart desires," said Zia Caterina.

"She never has to lift a finger. All she does is sit, looking out the window eating *dolci*"—sweets—said Zia Clorinda.

"Now that she is old enough to marry, Tony thinks that no man is good enough for his Serafina," the three sisters whispered to each other.

That *was* true. Tony did think that no man was worthy of
his darling daughter. He would not even talk to the young
men in the village who wanted to court Serafina.

So, poor Serafina would sit at the window behind the
curtains, eating her *dolci* and crying.

One day, Angelo, a wealthy nobleman from Milano, was
passing through the village. As he went by Tony's house, the
wind blew the curtains away from the window, and there sat
Serafina. Angelo and Serafina looked into each other's eyes
and it was love at first sight for both of them.

The three sisters were standing nearby. "Dear ladies,"
Angelo asked them, "who is that lovely creature sitting at that
window? *Che bella donna!*—What a beautiful woman! Is she
married or spoken for?"

"Ah, young *signore*," said Zia Clotilda. "That is Serafina, the daughter of Tony the baker. No, she is not married."

"And not likely to be for a long time," said Zia Caterina.

"No one is good enough for Tony's little Serafina," Zia Clorinda explained.

"Well, we'll see about that," said Angelo. "Now, aunties, tell me all you can about her."

The young nobleman and the three sisters sat and talked and talked and talked. And before long, Angelo knew all about Serafina and Tony the baker. And he knew all about Tony's dream of becoming the most famous baker in all of northern Italy.

"*Grazie,* aunties"—thank you—said Angelo. "I think I have a plan that will give Tony his dream and give me the wife of my dreams. But I will need your help. This is what I want you to do…."

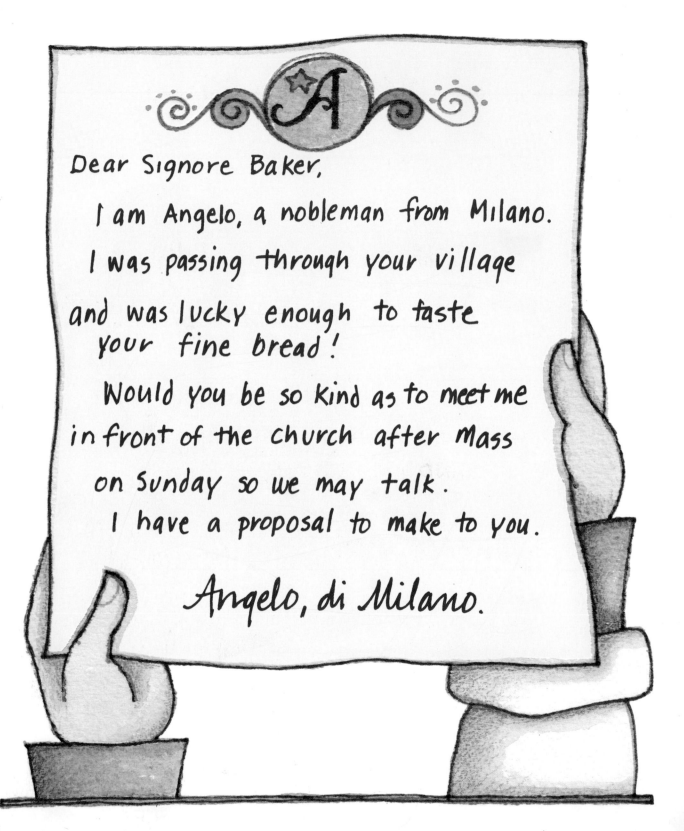

Dear Signore Baker,

I am Angelo, a nobleman from Milano.

I was passing through your village and was lucky enough to taste your fine bread!

Would you be so kind as to meet me in front of the church after Mass on Sunday so we may talk.

I have a proposal to make to you.

Angelo, di Milano.

and a secret letter arrived at Tony's house for Serafina.

Dear Bella Serafina, ♡ ♡ ♡

I saw you at your window and I love you!

Here's a ring to keep as a symbol
of my adoration.

It will not be long before we are
HUSBAND and WIFE!

♡Angelo, your true love.

And Zia Clotilda, Zia Caterina and Zia Clorinda did their part.

"Oh, Tony, did you see that rich young man from Milano?" Zia Clotilda asked.

"He wanted to know all about you. It seems he just loved your bread!" said Zia Caterina.

"Nothing like it in all Milano, he said," Zia Clorinda told Tony. "Why, I wouldn't be surprised if he wanted to meet you, the way he went on."

"Well, dear ladies, funny you should say that, because he does want to meet me—after Mass on Sunday," said Tony. "His name is Angelo di Milano."

"Imagine that!" the three women exclaimed. *"Che bella fortuna"*—What good luck for you. "And for Serafina!" they whispered to each other.

"And so, Signor Antonio, I would be most pleased if you and your lovely daughter would come to Milano as my guests," Angelo said.

"And if you like our city, I would be proud to set you up in a fine bakery of your own near the Piazza del Duomo— the cathedral square. Your fame would be assured, Signor Antonio. I will see to that."

Tony couldn't believe his ears. His dream was about to come true. "Why, thank you, Signor Angelo. But please, call me Tony. All my friends do."

"Also Signor Tony," Angelo continued. "The advantages for your beautiful daughter would be great. I admit I would not find it unpleasant for Serafina to sit beside me at my great table as my wife—the daughter of Tony, the most famous baker of Milano."

That did it! Tony agreed, and off he and Serafina went with Angelo. Together they walked all the small streets around the cathedral square and visited all the bakeries and pastry shops.

They tasted *torta*—cake—and *biscotti*—cookies—and *pane*—bread. And Tony was depressed. The bread alone was like nothing Tony had ever tasted: bread made out of the finest, whitest flour; bread shaped like pinwheels; bread with seeds of all sorts scattered over the top.

"It is no use, Signor Angelo," said a very sad Tony. "I can
never compete with all these fine bakeries and pastry shops.
All I can make is bread, and very simple bread at that.
I would be the laughingstock of Milano. It is better if
Serafina and I just go home."

"No, never!" Angelo shouted.

"Oh, Papa, no," Serafina cried. Not only was she in love
with Angelo, but she was looking forward to living in that
grand house with all those good things to eat.

"If only you could make bread that tasted as good and sweet as this candied fruit and these raisins," Serafina said.

"Or," Angelo said, getting another idea, "as rich and sweet as this cup of punch made from milk and eggs and honey!"

"Milk, eggs, honey," Tony said, thinking out loud.

"Candied fruit," Serafina said. "Raisins," Angelo chimed in.

"That's it!" all three shouted.

"I shall make the richest, lightest, most wonderful bread anyone has ever tasted—out of the whitest flour, the biggest eggs, the creamiest milk, the sweetest candied fruit and the plumpest raisins," Tony shouted.

"Oh, Papa," Serafina cried, kissing her father.

"Servants," Angelo called, and he sent them off to buy all the fine ingredients Tony would need.

The next morning, Tony, Serafina and all the supplies
headed back to the little village.

And Tony began to work. Day after day he experimented
until he had mixed the lightest, richest dough with as many
raisins and as much candied fruit as he could put into it.

Now he was ready to bake. He sent word to Angelo in
Milano that he should come to the bakery the next afternoon.
Then he set out the dough in large bowls and went
to bed. As Tony slept, the dough began to rise and rise and rise.

The next morning he filled every pan in his shop. One
piece of dough was left over so he threw it in a flower pot
and baked it too.

When Angelo arrived, the bread was just coming out of the oven. Everyone held his breath and waited while Tony cut a slice of his new bread. Angelo tasted it. Serafina tasted it. Tony tasted it. Zia Clotilda, Zia Caterina, Zia Clorinda all tasted it.

"That's it!" they shouted.

"I'll take these loaves back to Milano to see what my friends say," Angelo said, and off he went.

In just a few days a letter and a large cart filled with ingredients arrived in the village.

Dear Tony,
   Here are more supplies.
   Make as much bread as you can,
and send it to me.
   Then, when I send for you,
I promise you will enter Milano
with flags flying and Serafina
will be mine.
        Your future son-in-law,
              Angelo

P.S.
Please bake all the loaves in flowerpots.
My friends like the shape of that
loaf the best.

Just before Christmas, Angelo sent for Tony and Serafina.
Sure enough, when their coach entered Milano, crowds were
cheering and flags were flying.

"*Benvenuto, Tonio!*"—Welcome, Tony!—the crowds cheered.
"*Benvenuto!*"

The bishop and the mayor were there to greet Tony and
Serafina.

"And," said the mayor, "Milano is so happy to have you
here, so we may always have enough of your wonderful
bread!"

The next day when the bakery door was opened, the bishop's guards were called to keep order. All of Milano was there, except for Serafina and Angelo, who were being married quietly in a small chapel in the cathedral.

All during the wedding, they could hear the crowds cheering, calling for *pan di Tonio* — Tony's bread. And to this day, the *panettone* of Milano is eaten and enjoyed, especially at Christmas.

BRAVA SERAFINA, BRAVO ANGELO.
BRAVO TONY!